MORE WALKER PAPERBACKS
For You to Enjoy

ROSIE'S FISHING TRIP
by Amy Hest/Paul Howard

One morning very early Rosie and her grandad set off on a fishing trip together.
They have a fine time, but they don't come back with any fish!

"The harmony between the old and the very young has not often
been shown as effectively as it is here." *The Junior Bookshelf*

0-7445-4703-2　£4.99

THE WILD WOODS
by Simon James

When Jess takes a walk in the woods with Grandad, she discovers some
natural wonders and learns a lesson too about wild things.

"A breath of fresh air… Witty and sparkling line-and-wash pictures…
Full of humour and vitality." *The Guardian*

0-7445-3661-8　£4.99

THE TRAIN RIDE
by June Crebbin/Stephen Lambert

What could be finer than a train ride with Mum across country to the sea,
where someone very special is waiting – Grandma!

"There's lots to see, both on the bright red steam train and through its windows, with bold,
strongly coloured illustrations of a hazy summer's day sweeping across
the pages to draw you into the rhyme." *Practical Parenting*

0-7445-4701-6　£4.99

Walker Paperbacks are available from most booksellers, or by post from B.B.C.S., P.O. Box 941, Hull, North Humberside HU1 3YQ

24 hour telephone credit card line 01482 224626

To order, send: Title, author, ISBN number and price for each book ordered, your full name and address,
cheque or postal order payable to BBCS for the total amount and allow the following for postage and packing:
UK and BFPO: £1.00 for the first book, and 50p for each additional book to a maximum of £3.50.
Overseas and Eire: £2.00 for the first book, £1.00 for the second and 50p for each additional book.

Prices and availability are subject to change without notice.

Grandad Pot

SIOBHAN DODDS

WALKER BOOKS

AND SUBSIDIARIES

LONDON • BOSTON • SYDNEY

ring
ring
ring

"Hello, Grandad Pot. Mummy said I could come to tea and stay the night and if I'm good you might make me a chocolate cake. Chocolate cake is my favourite food. Don't worry, Grandad Pot – I won't be any trouble."

What a surprise for Grandad Pot! Polly is coming to stay.

Quick, quick, quick!
A chocolate cake for Polly.

ring
ring
ring

"Hello, Grandad Pot.
Can Henry come too?
He won't be any trouble.
Henry has a big plaster
on his knee. He was
doing cartwheels in the garden and he
fell over. He didn't cry. He told me that
jelly and ice-cream will make his knee
better. Don't worry, Grandad Pot.
Henry can sleep in my bed."

What a surprise for
Grandad Pot!
Henry is coming
to stay.

Quick, quick, quick!
Jelly and ice-cream for Henry.
Oh! and a chocolate cake
for Polly.

ring
ring
ring

"Hello, Grandad Pot.
Can Rosie come too?
She won't be any trouble.
Rosie isn't feeling very
well today. I think she
has a cold. She sneezed four
times this morning. She likes
banana sandwiches best. Don't worry,
Grandad Pot. Rosie can
sleep in my bed too."

What a surprise for
Grandad Pot! Rosie
is coming
to stay.

Quick, quick, quick!
Banana sandwiches for Rosie.
Jelly and ice-cream for Henry.
Oh! and a chocolate cake
for Polly.

ring
ring
ring

"Hello, Grandad Pot.
Can George come too?
He won't be any trouble.
George has red spotted
shorts and a big, fat tummy.
His favourite food is sausages.
Don't worry, Grandad Pot.
George can sleep in
my bed too."

What a surprise
for Grandad Pot!
George is
coming
to stay.

Quick, quick, quick!
Sausages for George.
Banana sandwiches for Rosie.
Jelly and ice-cream for Henry.
Oh! and a chocolate cake
for Polly.

Knock
Knock
Knock

"Hello, Grandad Pot.
This is Henry,
this is Rosie,
and this is George."

What a surprise
for Grandad Pot!
Oh! and ...

what an enormous tea for Polly!

"Goodnight, Grandad Pot.
It's lots of fun coming to stay."

For Nana and Grandad

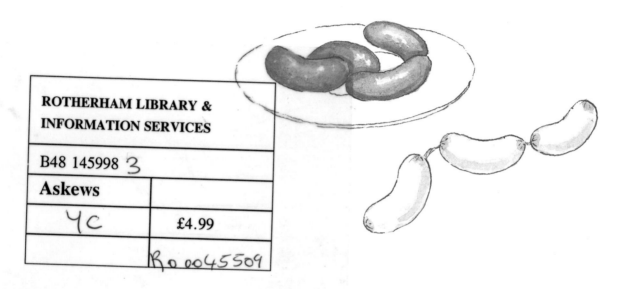

First published 1993 by Walker Books Ltd
87 Vauxhall Walk, London SE11 5HJ

This edition published 2003

2 4 6 8 10 9 7 5 3 1

©1993 Siobhan Dodds

The right of Siobhan Dodds to be identified
as author/illustrator of this work has been
asserted by her in accordance with the
Copyright, Designs and Patents Act 1988

This book has been typeset in Garamond

Printed in China

British Library Cataloguing in Publication Data:
a catalogue record for this book is available
from the British Library

ISBN 0-7445-9814-1